Let's all go to the PUMPKIN PATCH

Kristen Hanson

Co-Author: Grayson Shovlin

Copyright © 2022 Kristen Hanson and Grayson Shovlin
All rights reserved
First Edition

NEWMAN SPRINGS PUBLISHING
320 Broad Street
Red Bank, NJ 07701

First originally published by Newman Springs Publishing 2022

ISBN 978-1-68498-308-7 (Paperback)
ISBN 978-1-68498-309-4 (Digital)

Printed in the United States of America

To my four kids, Grayson, Eastyn, Owen, and Cameron, and my husband, Cory. They've given me the best job on earth—being a stay-at-home mom and getting to have endless adventures with the ones I love most. Also, to my mom and dad who gave me a fun-filled childhood with tons of adventures and memories to be able to pass on to my own little ones.

To the Vala family - for creating my ultimate childhood experience at Vala's Pumpkin Patch and continuing to keep the magic alive each fall so I can continue making memories with the ones I love. Especially to Jan Vala, Co-Founder of Vala's Pumpkin Patch. She loved reading with children and I hope my children's book can honor her and the masterpiece she helped create!

Hooray, hooray, it's time to play!
We've waited all year for opening day!

Arriving early to get in line,
Get ready y'all, it's pumpkin patch time!

Walking shoes on, ready to explore,
We're finally through the entrance door!

Graveyard golf and a huge rocking chair!
Off to the haunted house... time for a scare!

The Haunted Farmhouse gives us shivers and shakes,
Skeletons dancing and glowing-eyed snakes!

Holding hands tightly, dim lights turning black,
A mysterious sound gives a click and a clack!

We start running through, as fast as can be,
Arrive at the end and we're finally free!

On to explore the haunted trails,
Then Bunnyville to visit the cottontails!

The leaves are changing with colors so pretty,
It feels so good to escape the city.

Dirt paths and gravel roads,
Our senses are on overload!

Scenes are full of reds and yellows,
Crisp bonfires and toasted marshmallows!

Tractor rides and a loop on the train,
Nothing but goblins and ghosts on the brain!

Endless kettle corn and huge milkshakes,
Enough to give us bellyaches!

Tractor sandbox, hayrack rides,
Flying down the tallest slides!

Corn pit, ponies, the lost pumpkin mine,
Feeling so free cruising on the zip line!

Apple blasters and pumpkin picking,
All the pies are finger-licking!

Chocolate chip cookies and caramel apples,
Winning paintball in epic battles!

Carousel rides and cider slushes,
Bubble wands and pumpkin plushies!

Turkey legs as big as the sun,
And apple donuts on the run!

The wooden playhouses are the best,
Then off to have a pirate quest!

We ride the ship then jump in the hay,
Today might be my favorite day!

Apple picking is next on the list,
They pluck off the trees with a flip of the wrist!

So many to chose from—red, yellow, green,
Granny Smith, Gala and more in between!

Into the cornstalks to conquor the maze,
It's at the pumpkin patch I have the best days!

There's pumpkins for picking and pumpkins for baking,
Pumpkins are grown just for the taking.
For us to carve and to eat,
And to light up when we trick-or-treat.

While pumpkin patch season may come and pass,
Our adventures and memories are built to last!

About the Author

Meet the author of this book. She is currently a stay-at-home mom and owns her own small business doing planters and custom floral designs. Her true dream has always been to raise her children, and she's doing it with a grateful heart. They spend their days on endless adventures, exploring at the farm, apple orchard, and zoo, but nothing beats the pumpkin patch and all things autumn! Kristen grew up going to the pumpkin patch every fall with her family and is so excited that she gets to share that family tradition with her own kids. There isn't a better way to spend a crisp autumn morning or evening than under the orange pumpkin lights at the best place on earth! It's truly her second home and what her family lives for each fall season! They're at the pumpkin patch opening day each September and spend as many of their days and nights there as their busy schedule allows! Kristen hopes to instill lasting memories and traditions for her children to share with their own kids in the future!

Printed in the USA
CPSIA information can be obtained
at www.ICGtesting.com
LVHW070019250924
791985LV00013B/121